This book belongs to

Curious George's 5-Minute Stories

INSPIRED AND CREATED BY
MARGRET AND H. A. REY

HOUGHTON MIFFLIN HARCOURT
Boston New York

Contents

Curious George
Visits the Library

This is George. He was a good little monkey and always very curious. Today George and his friend the man with the yellow hat were at the library. George had never been to the library before. He had never seen so many books before, either.

Everywhere he looked, people were reading. Some people read quietly to themselves. But in the children's room the librarian

was reading out loud. It was story hour! George loved stories. He
sat down with a group of children to listen.

The librarian was reading a book about a bunny. George liked bunnies. Behind the librarian was a book about a dinosaur. George liked dinosaurs even more. He hoped she would read it next.

But next the librarian read a book about a train. George tried to sit quietly and wait for the dinosaur book to be read. But sometimes it is hard for a little monkey to be patient.

When the librarian started a story about jungle animals, George could not wait any longer. He had to see the dinosaur book. He tiptoed closer.

"Look, a monkey!" shouted a girl.

The librarian put her finger to her lips. "We must be quiet so everyone can hear," she said nicely.

"But there's a monkey!" said a boy.

The librarian nodded and smiled. "Mmm-hmm," she agreed.

When she finished reading the jungle story, the librarian reached for the dinosaur book. Where did it go? And where was George?

George was all ready to take the dinosaur book home and read it with his friend when another book caught his eye. The book was about trucks. George wanted to take it home, too!

And here was a book about elephants. George loved elephants. He added it to his pile. George found so many good books, he soon had more than he could carry. He leaned against a shelf to rest.

Squeak, went the shelf.

"Shhh!" said a man.

Squeak, went the shelf again—and it moved! Why, it wasn't really a shelf after all. George had found a special cart for carrying books. What luck! Now George could carry all the books he wanted.

He rolled the cart between the shelves and stacked up books about boats and kites and baking cakes. He climbed higher to reach books about cranes and planes.

At last George had all the books he could handle. He couldn't wait to head home and start reading. And right in front of him was a ramp leading to the door. George was curious. Could he roll the cart all the way home? Down the ramp George went. The cart rolled faster and faster.

"Stop!" a library volunteer shouted. "Come back here with my cart!"

But George was too excited to listen. The cart was picking up speed, and George was having fun! Until—CRASH!—George and the cart ran smack into a shelf of encyclopedias. Books flew up in the air. And so did George! He landed in a big pile right between O and P.

"Oh no!" moaned the volunteer when he saw the mess George had made. "How am I going to put away all of these books?"

"I'd like to borrow this one," said a boy from story hour.

"And I'll take this one," said a girl.

With help from George and the children, the books were sorted in no time. Soon there was just a small pile of George's favorites left.

"Would you like to take those books home with you?" the volunteer asked George. Then he took George to a special desk and helped him get his very own library card.

George was holding his brand-new card when his friend arrived with a stack of books of his own. "There you are, George!" he said. "I see you are all ready to check out." George and his friend gave their books to the librarian.

She smiled when she saw George's pile. "I was wondering where this dinosaur book went," she said. "It's one of my favorites, too." The librarian stamped the books and handed them back to George.

With his books under one arm, George waved goodbye to the volunteer, the librarian, and the children from story hour.

"Come see us again, George," the librarian said, waving back. "Enjoy your books!"

And he did.

Curious George
Marches in the Parade

This is George. He was a good little monkey and always very curious. This morning, George woke up to find a flag attached to his bedpost. He was curious at first, but then he remembered.

It was Celebrate Our Town Day, and there was going to be a picnic! There was going to be a parade!

"Good morning, George," said the man with the yellow hat. "Are you ready for Celebrate Our Town Day?"

George packed his wagon with everything he would need: his flag, his picnic basket full of delicious snacks, and his little trumpet, of course.

"Time to go, George," said the man. George could hardly wait.

Everyone in town was heading to the park for the celebration.
George and the man met some friends on the street. They had
flags and picnic baskets too! George was very impatient to
go-go-*GO*, but he remembered to wait for the red light before
crossing the street.

Finally, they arrived at the park. "Are you hungry, George?" asked the man. "We have all the good snacks you packed. Let's eat before we play."

George felt impatient again. He wanted to climb trees! But he was also feeling hungry.

He and the man had a delicious picnic. They ate juicy plums and sweet homemade pie, and gulped down cups of cool lemonade.

George licked every last crumb from all ten fingers and toes, and then he was ready. Play time!

George couldn't pick just one game, so he played them all. He climbed up a lamppost (like only a monkey can) to catch a wild Frisbee. He played some jacks, and he only dropped a few. He won a game of hopscotch in three seconds flat. Monkeys are very good at hopping.

At the playground, George slid down the slide in a blur of fur— *whoosh!*—and spun his friends on the merry-go-round. Maybe just a *little* too fast.

Then, it was time for the parade. George and the man and all
of their friends found a spot on the sidewalk to watch. It was a good
spot, but George thought he would be able to see better from higher
up. He was very impatient to see the float and the band. He could
hear them playing, but he couldn't . . . quite . . . see them.

So he climbed and climbed up a tree (as only a monkey can),

and—look! He could see the float with Lady Liberty riding tall. He could see the band and hear their happy tune. He could see the pretty white horse prancing at the front of the line.

George was very happy with his watching spot until—*crack!*— the branch broke! Down George fell. He landed with a crash. The sound frightened the horse. The horse threw her rider. The rider ran after the horse. The horse barreled into the float, and Lady Liberty toppled into the street. The parade was ruined.

George felt awful.

George thought and thought. There had to be a way to clean up the mess. He was very impatient for a good idea—and then he had one!

He needed a dress, some stars, and some string. Something for a torch—an ice cream cone, of course!

And, last but not least, the horse. Luckily, she was as impatient for a snack as George was to get the parade started again.

Finally, everything was ready. Lady Liberty held her torch high. The band took their places and tuned their instruments. The acrobats stretched and twirled. The clown did tricks while the fire chief and his Dalmatian took their places.

George jumped up on the horse and waited patiently for everyone to find their places. Then he blew his whistle and away they went!

It was a beautiful parade. At last!

Curious George
Goes Fishing

This is George. He was a good little monkey and always very curious.

One day George was playing when he saw something funny. He saw a long string on a long stick being carried by a big man. What could the man be doing with a string on a stick?

George was curious.

The man was on his way to the lake, and soon George was on his way to the lake too.

George watched the man put a hook on the end of the string and a piece of food on the hook. Then the man lowered the string into the water and waited. When the man pulled the string out of the water, there was a big fish on the hook.

What fun it must be to fish! George wanted to fish too.

He had a string. All he needed was a stick. And he knew just
where to get one. George ran home as fast as he could.

A mop would make a good stick. George tied his string to the mop. Now he was all set to fish.

Or was he?

Not yet.

George had to have a hook, and on the hook something that
fish like to eat. Fish would like cake, and George knew where to find
some. But where could he get a hook? Why, there was a hook on the
wall! It would have to come out.

With the hook on the string and the string on the stick and the cake in a box in his hand, George went back to the lake. He put some cake on the hook and lowered the string into the water. Now he had to wait.

Would he catch anything on the end of his string? George was curious. The fish were curious too. All kinds of fish came to look at the string—big fish and little fish, red fish and yellow fish and blue fish. One of them was near the hook. The cake was just what he wanted.

George waited.

The string shook.

But when George pulled the string up, there was no fish on the hook, and there was no cake on the hook either. The fish had just taken the cake and swum away!

Well, if George could not get the fish, the fish would not get the cake. George would eat it. The cake was just what he wanted too. He would find another way to fish.

George looked into the water. A big red fish with a long tail was so near. Could he reach it? Could he catch a fish without a string? George got down as low as he could and put out his hand.

SPLASH! Into the lake he went! The water was cold and wet.

George was cold and wet too. This was no fun at all.

When George got out of the water, his friend Bill was there with his kite. "My, you are wet!" Bill said. "I saw you fall in, so I came to help you get out. Too bad you did not get a fish! But it is good the fish did not get you. Maybe now you can help me fly my kite."

George was happy to help. It was a windy day, and soon
George was dry and the kite was flying high. He watched it go
up and up and up. What fun it was to fly a kite!

It would have been fun to catch a fish on the end of a string, thought George, but flying a kite on the end of a string was even better.

Curious George Says Thank You

This is George. He was a good little monkey and always very curious.

Today George received a surprise in the mail. "It looks like you got a card, George," said the man with the yellow hat. It was a thank-you card from George's neighbor Betsy.

The card made George smile. It also made him curious. Who could he give a thank-you card to? George thought and thought.

He could send one to the science museum director, Dr. Lee, who had shown George her favorite collection of dinosaur fossils. Of course, there was also the librarian who helped him pick out books. Hmm . . . The store clerk at the market always saved the

best bananas for him. And his friend Bill let George fly his kite in the park.

George had so many people to thank he had to get started right away! First he gathered paper, envelopes, crayons, and stickers. Then he got to work. The man with the yellow hat walked in to find George covered from head to toe.

"Uh-oh, George! What are you doing?"

George held up Betsy's card and pointed to the papers scattered around him.

"Oh, I see, George," said his friend. "You're making your own thank-you cards. What a nice idea. Would you like some help?"

The man wrote while George decorated. George was having so much fun that they even made a stack of extra cards.

"We can hand-deliver these tomorrow. Everyone will be happy to see you, George."

Their first stop was the science museum.

"George, it's so good to see you," said Dr. Lee. "What a lovely card! I'm going to hang it in my office right now."

Next they stopped at the library. "What a great card," the librarian said. "I'm going to set it here on my desk where everyone can see it. George, we have some new books in the children's section that you might like, if you have time."

George looked at his friend. "All right," the man said. "I will go get a book for myself."

George noticed the mail carrier leaving the library. She was the one who had brought George his thank-you card in the first place.

He wanted to give her one of his cards too! George hurried out the door. Could he catch her in time?

George jumped up and down on the steps, waving a card, but a group of children was just getting off a bus. They were coming to the library for story hour. George couldn't see which way the mail carrier had gone. But, oh! There was a streetlight nearby. George was curious. Maybe if he climbed it, he could see where the mail carrier was going.

George started to climb the streetlight as fast as only a monkey can. But when he was halfway up the pole, his bag slipped off. In an instant, all of George's thank-you cards went whirling through the air.

Oh, no! How would George deliver his cards now?
George slid down the pole and grabbed at the cards
swirling around him.

A boy looked up. "Hey! It's snowing mail!"

A little girl said, "Don't worry, little monkey. We'll help you pick up your cards."

The children gathered up the cards. George was very grateful for their help. He was also grateful that he had brought extra cards.

He decided to give them to all of the children.

"These cards are so nice!" said the teacher.

The man with the yellow hat came hurrying down the steps. "George! I didn't see you leave. It looks like you've had quite an adventure out here." The man thanked the teacher and his students for helping George.

"Let's finish delivering those thank-you cards," said the man. George and his friend stopped by the market and the park and then headed home.

George felt a little sad that he hadn't caught up to the mail carrier. But wait! Who was that at George's house?

George proudly gave her a thank-you card.

"Wow, George!" said the mail carrier. "I'm usually the one delivering the cards. This sure is a treat!"

George waved goodbye, and he and the man went into their house. But George had one more very special thank-you card to deliver. He had saved the best for last!

Curious George
at the Baseball Game

This is George. He was a good little monkey and always very curious.

Today George and the man with the yellow hat were going to the ballpark to watch a baseball game. George couldn't wait to see what it would be like.

At the baseball stadium, the man with the yellow hat introduced George to his friend, the head coach of the Mudville Miners. He had arranged for George to watch the game from the dugout. What a treat! George got a Miners cap to wear. Then he sat on the bench with the players. He felt just like part of the team!

The players cheered a Miners home run. George cheered too. The players groaned at a Miners strikeout. George groaned too.

Then George noticed one of the Miners coaches making funny motions with his hands. He touched his cap. He pinched his nose. He dusted off his shoulder.

Hmm, thought George. Maybe this was another way to cheer on the team. So George made some hand motions too. He tugged at his ear. He rubbed his tummy. He scratched his chin.

Just then, a Miners player got tagged out at second base. The player pointed at George. "That monkey!" he said. "He distracted me with his funny signs."

Oops! The coach had been giving directions to the base runner. George's hand signals had taken his mind off the play. Poor George! He had only been trying to be part of the team. Instead the Miners had lost a chance to score.

George watched the rest of the game from a stadium seat. Or at least he tried to watch the game. There was so much going on around him. There was food for sale. There were shouting fans. There was a woman holding a big camera . . .

The woman pointed her camera at some fans. And look! Those fans waved out from the huge screen on the ballpark scoreboard. George had never been on TV before. He was very curious. What would it be like to see himself on the big screen? He soon learned the answer: it was exciting! George liked seeing himself up there.

"Hey, you!" shouted the camerawoman. "Cut that out!"

Uh-oh! George had gotten a little carried away. He ran off, with the angry camerawoman hot on his heels. In the busy stadium breezeway, George hid behind a popcorn cart. He waited for the camerawoman to pass by.

Just then, George heard a noise behind him. It was a quiet little noise—like a sigh, or a sniff. What could have made that noise? George wondered. George turned. There, behind the cart, was a little boy, crying. George wanted to help. He crept out of his hiding place and over to the boy.

"Ah-ha! There you are!" shouted the camerawoman, spotting George. Then the camerawoman noticed the teary-eyed boy. She seemed to forget that she was mad at George.

"I'm lost," the boy said. "I can't find my dad."

If only there was a way to let the boy's dad know where he was.

But there was a way! The camerawoman aimed her lens at the little

boy, and . . .

there he was on the big screen for everyone to see — including

his dad.

Within minutes, the boy and his father were together again and the man with the yellow hat had come to find George.

"I can't thank you enough," the boy's father said to the camerawoman.

The camerawoman shrugged. "Don't thank me," she said. She patted George on the head. "It was this little fellow who found your son."

George was the star of the day.

Curious George
and the Bunny

This is George. George was a good little monkey and always very curious.

One day George found a little house. Inside was a big white bunny and a lot of little bunnies.

George looked and looked. Bunnies were something new to him. He wondered what it would feel like to hold one.

The big bunny was the Mother Bunny. She was as big as George. But the little bunnies were so little that George could hold them in his hand.

How could he get a bunny out of the house? A house must have a door to get in and to get out. Oh—there it was! George put his hand in and took out a baby bunny. It was fun to hold a baby bunny! And the bunny did not seem to mind.

Now he and the bunny could play a game in the garden. They could play Get the Bunny. George would let the bunny hop away, and then he would run after it and get it back. He put the bunny down . . . but the bunny ran off like a shot! Where did the bunny go?

George looked and looked, but the bunny was gone. All the fun was gone too. George was sad. Now he could not put the bunny back in the house with Mother Bunny.

Why, that was it! George had an idea. Mother Bunny could help him! All he needed was a bit of string.

He ran to the bunny house and tied the string
to the Mother Bunny. She knew just what to do. Away she
went with her head down and her ears up. All George could do was
hold on tight and run!

George followed Mother Bunny. Soon she saw something. George saw it too!

George and Mother Bunny ran and ran. And then Mother Bunny sat down. George saw the baby bunny's tail poking out of a hole. A bunny likes to dig a hole and then go down and lie in it. But this bunny was too little to live in a hole. It belonged in a bunny house, and that was where George took it.

The baby bunny followed its mother all the way home. George didn't even have to tie a string on it. When they returned to the bunny house, Mother Bunny and all the little baby bunnies lay down to sleep.

George was glad to see Mother Bunny and all her babies safe and sound.

Good night, bunnies!

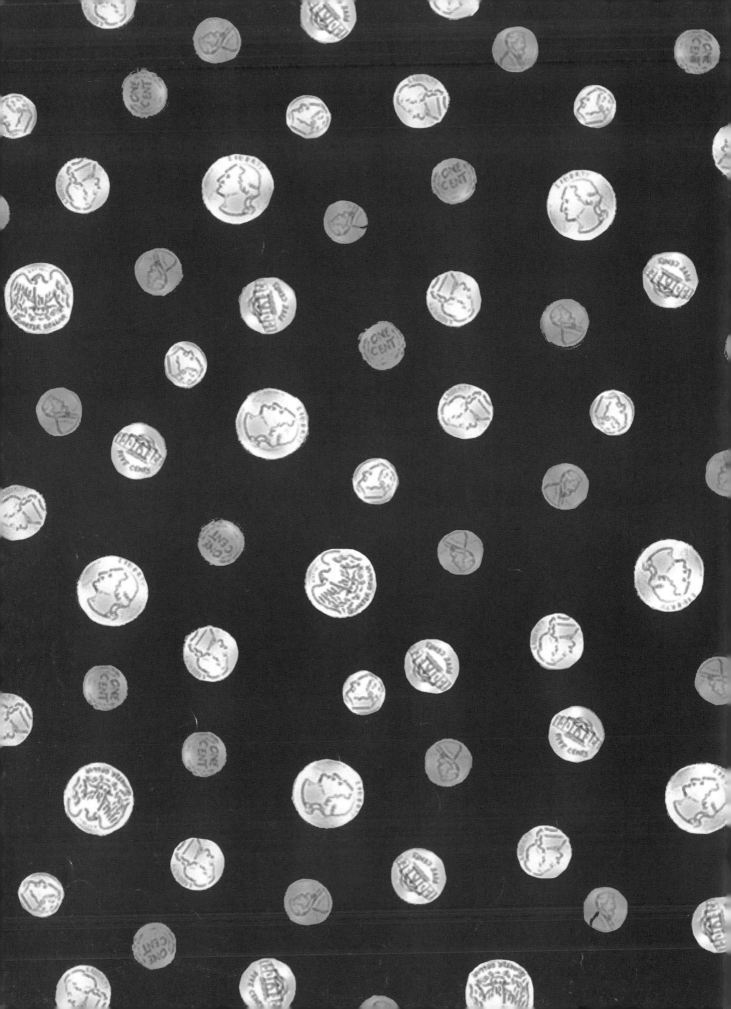

Curious George
Saves His Pennies

George was a good little monkey and always very curious, especially

when he was in Tammy's Toy Store.

There were so many things to wonder about . . . pogo sticks and skateboards, snow globes and kaleidoscopes, and even finger traps.

But George's favorite thing to do in the toy store was play at the train table. Today there was a new train. Its wood was painted bright red, and it had a real working whistle. George showed it to his friend, the man with the yellow hat.

"Not today," his friend said. "We're looking for a birthday present for Noah, remember? He's turning five. "

George helped his friend pick out a yellow and green hula hoop. While Tammy the shopkeeper wrapped the present for the birthday party, George wandered back to the train table.

"I have a suggestion, George," said the man as he carried the gift over. "Why don't you buy that new train yourself? The tag says $5.00. I'm sure you can save the money for it." George liked this suggestion so much that he was only a little sorry to put the train back down.

George had a good time at the birthday party. Noah let everyone have a turn at the hula hoop. It was harder than it looked!

As soon as George got home that afternoon, he took his piggy bank down from his dresser. He opened the small plug at the bottom and shook. Out tumbled a nickel. George ran to show the coin to his friend.

"You have five cents," the man said. "I'll give you your allowance early this week. Don't spend it on candy. You have to save it up." The man gave George two quarters. "Here is fifty cents," he said. "Now you have fifty-five cents. You have only four dollars and forty-five cents left to save." George wasn't quite sure how much money that was, but it sounded like a lot.

George dreamed about his red train that night. He was riding it through a forest of trees. He tugged on the whistle again and again so that no one could miss such a shiny red engine!

In the morning, George decided he would have to find a way to earn money faster. What if someone else were to buy the red train at the toy store before he could? He had an idea.

George found five pennies and a dime in the sofa cushions. He found a nickel under his bed. His piggy bank jingled nicely that evening. He had seventy-five cents saved. One more quarter and he would have a dollar!

The next morning George had another idea. He would get a job. Lucky for George, his neighbor Mr. Reddy needed help raking leaves. George worked all morning long, gathering armfuls of red, brown, and gold leaves to add to a growing pile in the center of the yard. Mr. Reddy brought out lemonade for the two to share. While his neighbor rested on the sun porch swing, George climbed a tree.

The pile of leaves looked tempting from above. George wondered what would happen if . . . Before he finished wondering, he had swung out of the branches and right into the center of the pile. The leaves crunched and crumbled and swooshed and swirled. What an adventure!

What hard work it was raking the leaves back up!

But at the end of the day, Mr. Reddy paid him two dollars. George had $2.75 saved. That was almost three dollars.

George spent many days doing odd jobs. He washed windows. He distributed flyers. He delivered flowers. He did dishes. At the end of a week, George finally had $5.00.

"I'm proud of you, George," said the man with the yellow hat. "You saved all that money by yourself. You've sure earned that train."

The change clinked merrily in the piggy bank as George set off for the toy store. The autumn day was bright and clear. George walked

by the park. The neighborhood children were playing with a windsock. Suddenly, it got stuck in a tree. They needed George's help!

George carefully set his piggy bank down on a nearby park bench where he could keep an eye on it. But little monkeys sometimes forget.

As George went from helping to playing, he forgot to check that his bank was still there. As the afternoon wore on, his friends went home to have dinner. George rushed to the park bench where he had left his piggy bank. The toy store might be closing soon. But his bank was gone!

Maybe George had the wrong bench? There were many in the park, after all. But he was disappointed each time he ran up to another empty bench.

George walked home sadly. He wondered how long it would take him to save five dollars again.

As George passed the toy store, he happened to look through the window. He couldn't believe his eyes. A little girl was holding his piggy bank! George rushed into the toy store just as the girl's mother was saying, "We found this across the street and waited for its owner, but it's getting late. We saw it has the name of your store on the bottom. Can you keep it in case someone comes to claim it?"

George jumped up and down on the counter. "Why, George!" Tammy said. "Is the piggy bank yours? You're lucky Hana and her mother found it."

Hugging his piggy bank tightly, George rushed over to the train section. He located the shiny red engine right away. As he carried it to the counter, the little girl looked at his train shyly.

George realized he had not said thank you to her for keeping his savings safe. He looked at his train. He looked at his piggy bank. He looked at Hana. Good deeds deserve to be rewarded, he decided.

George set the train down. He upended his bank on the counter and began to sort dollars and coins. George and Hana walked out of the toy store that day each carrying a train. George's small engine was not red, but it was shiny and blue and he had paid for it all by himself. Best of all, he had a new friend who loved to play with trains almost as much as he did.

Curious George
at the Aquarium

This is George. He was a good little monkey and always very curious.

Today George and the man with the yellow hat were visiting the aquarium.

"George," said the man, "please wait here while I buy the tickets."

George tried to wait, but he was so excited! What was inside? He wanted to look over the walls, but they were too high.

Just then, he heard a *SPLASH!* and a *WHOOSH!* Water flew high into the air. People cheered. What could that be? George was curious. He hopped over the wall into the aquarium. How surprised he was!

Swimming right in front of George were two beluga whales! The mother and the baby beluga whale swam right past him. And not far away was a family of sea lions, diving and splashing.

What fun! George noticed people walking toward a big door—could there be more to see? He followed the crowd.

Now where was he? It was darker inside and there were fish everywhere! George did not know where to look first. In one tank there were sharp-toothed piranhas, in another tank there were sea horses, and in another tank there was a large red octopus!

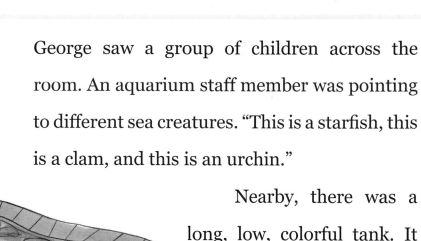

George saw a group of children across the room. An aquarium staff member was pointing to different sea creatures. "This is a starfish, this is a clam, and this is an urchin."

Nearby, there was a long, low, colorful tank. It was perfect for touching! George was curious. As he reached his hand into the water, a large crab came scuttling out from under a rock and right toward his finger!

Snap! Ouch! Poor George. He did not like this exhibit.

George slipped out a door into the sunlight. But, oh! What was going on here? George saw fat, funny-looking black and white fish swimming under the water. As he watched they flew up out of the water. What kind of fish

does that, and where did they go? George wondered. George climbed up and into their exhibit.

They were not fish at all, but penguins, of course!

George hopped like a penguin, flapped his wings like a penguin, and waddled like a penguin. A crowd gathered and laughed. But when he slid on his belly like a penguin . . .

The aquarium staff stopped by to check on the penguins. "A monkey! In the penguin exhibit?"

George opened a door to escape, but instead . . . the penguins ran out! Penguins, penguins everywhere! The staff was angry at George. How could they catch all the penguins?

In the excitement nobody noticed the penguin chick falling into the water! No one but George. The baby penguin hadn't learned

to swim yet. As only a monkey can, George scaled the rope hanging over the beluga tank and swung over the water, saving the chick.

The director of the aquarium and the man with the yellow hat heard the commotion and came running.

"That monkey helped the baby penguin," said a boy in the crowd.

"No one else could have saved him," said a girl.

The director thanked George for his help and made him an honorary staff member of the aquarium.

George said goodbye to his new penguin friends. He could not wait to come back to the aquarium and visit again!

Curious George Blasts Off!

This is George. He was a good little monkey and always very curious.

One day George got an important letter. George's friend, the man with the yellow hat, helped him read it.

MUSEUM OF SCIENCE

Dear George,

A small space ship has been built by our experimental station. It is too small for a man but could carry a little monkey. Would you be willing to go up in it?

I have never met you but I hear that you are a bright little monkey who can do all sorts of things, and that is just what we need.

We want you to do something nobody has ever done before: bail out of a space ship in flight.

When we flash you a signal you will have to open the door and bail out with the help of emergency rockets.

We hope that you are willing and that your friend will permit you to go.

Gratefully yours
Professor Wiseman
Director of the Science Museum.

"George," he said, "Professor Wiseman needs your help for an experiment. He's built a rocket ship to travel into space. It is too small for a person to ride in, but it is just the right size for a clever monkey."

George thought and thought. He had never been to space before, but he was very curious about it.

"Do you want to go into space, George? You will have to be very brave . . ."

George was glad to help. George and his friend set out for the museum at once to talk to the professor and meet the other scientists.

"We are so happy you are willing to help us, George!" said

Professor Wiseman. "Let's gather everything you need for your flight."

They got the smallest size space suit for George, along with a space helmet, an oxygen tank, emergency rockets, and a parachute. They helped him put everything on and taught him how to use it all.

When everything was ready, a truck drove up with a special screen mounted on it to watch the flight. Everyone got on, and they were off to the launching site!

They checked all the controls of the spaceship, especially the lever that opened the door. George tried it too. He was very excited to go to space, but he was excited to come home too!

Finally, the great moment had come. George knew just what to do. He went aboard the spaceship and waved goodbye. Then . . .

Five—

four—

three—

two—

one—

BLASTOFF!

The ship rose faster and higher and higher, until the scientists could no longer see it in the sky. But on the screen they saw George clearly all the time.

Now the moment had come for George to bail out of the ship. Professor Wiseman flashed the signal. Everyone watched the screen. George did not move. Why didn't he pull the lever? In a few seconds it would be too late. The ship would be lost in outer space with George in it!

Everyone watching on the ground waited and waited. They were nervous— especially George's friend, the man with the yellow hat.

Then, slowly, George began to move onscreen. He reached for a lever and the door opened at last.

Out of the blue an open parachute came floating down to earth.
Hurrah—George was on his way back home!

The truck raced to the spot where he would land. What a
welcome for George!

Professor Wiseman hung a big golden medal around his neck.

"Because," he said, "you are the first astronaut to fly into space and come back to earth."

On the medal it said: TO GEORGE, THE FIRST SPACE MONKEY.

The newspaper man took George's picture, and everybody shouted and cheered—the man in the yellow hat most of all.

"I'm proud of you, George," he said. "I guess the whole world is proud of you today."

It was the happiest day in George's life.

Curious George
Goes to the Zoo

This is George. George was a good little monkey and always very curious. Today, George was feeling very excited. The man with the yellow hat was taking him to the zoo!

As they drove, the man explained to George that this wasn't just any zoo that they were going to visit.

"It's called the Wild Animal Park," the man said. "All of the animals roam around freely."

When they arrived, George saw a huge banner. George looked up at it, but he could not read the words.

A friendly zookeeper explained. "It's an extra-special day here at the Wild Animal Park," she said. "It is our baby rhino's first birthday. We are going to have a party for her later on!"

A party! This was going to be a wonderful trip to the zoo.

George tried to walk into the park where the animals were, but the zookeeper stopped him. "You can't walk in there!" she said. "To explore this zoo, you have to ride in one of our special cars."

She pointed to a huge car that had no roof on it.

Oh, my! What fun this was going to be. George and his friend climbed onboard and the car drove into the park.

Soon they were in the midst of the Wild Animal Park. "Look over there!" said the zookeeper. "There's our pride of lions. We have a large family here."

George pointed in the other direction. "Yes, George," said the zookeeper. "I see the giraffes too. Their tall necks help them eat leaves from the treetops. And there are two ostriches running this way!" George was happy to be seeing so many amazing animals.

The zoo car drove past a small pond. Pink flamingos waded in the water. Their heads bobbed up and down as they walked on spindly legs. "The flamingos turn pink because they eat so many tiny pink shrimp," said the zookeeper, but George was not listening.

He had never seen flamingos before. He was curious about how those flamingos were moving. He leaned out the back of the zoo car as far as he could to take a look. But then—oh! What happened?

First George lost his balance. Then he fell—*kerplunk!*—right out of the zoo car. His friend hadn't noticed that he had fallen. George ran as quickly as a little monkey could toward the pond.

The flamingos bobbed their heads and lifted their feet one at a time. It looked like they were dancing. George danced with them.

Suddenly, the water in the pond started to move. Then a hippo popped its head out from under the water. What a surprise! George stopped dancing to take a look.

The hippo opened its huge mouth as if it were yawning. George opened his mouth wide too. It was fun to act like the hippo! Just then, George noticed that something was rustling in the reeds near

the pond. George was curious. He wanted to see what was there. In an instant, he jumped over the reeds. He poked his nose inside and saw . . . a baby rhino!

The tiny rhino was cute, but she looked a little bit sad and a little bit lonely. George wanted to make that baby rhino feel happy again. He thought and thought. Maybe the baby rhino would like the flamingo dance. He jumped and bobbed his head and danced

his feet up and down. The baby rhino peeked her head out of the reeds so that she could watch. George danced more, and the rhino walked out of the reeds. She was curious too!

They were having so much fun that George didn't notice

what was behind him. The zookeeper stomped over to George. She did not look happy. The man with the yellow hat was running behind her.

"You are a naughty little monkey," said the zookeeper. "You were supposed to stay in the car. You and your friend will have to go now."

George walked to the man's side. He waved goodbye to the baby rhino. The man and the zookeeper turned to see whom George was waving to.

"The baby rhino! Why, we've been looking for her all day," said the zookeeper. "She got separated from her mother."

George was glad to see the zookeeper looking happy again. He and the man started walking toward the exit. The zookeeper ran to stop them.

"Thank you for finding our baby rhino, George. And just in time for her birthday party. Will you join us for some cake?" George jumped with glee. He had forgotten about the party, and he did love cake.

The man and George followed the zookeeper and the baby rhino back to zoo headquarters. The rhino's mother was waiting there for her. The zookeeper brought out a special birthday cake that was shaped like a rhino. George had never seen a cake that was shaped like that before.

"You can have the first piece, George," said the zookeeper. "I also have a special treat, just for you!" She placed a bunch of bananas in front of him. George was very happy to have a tasty banana, but he saved room for some cake, too!

Curious George
and the Ice Cream Surprise

George was a good little monkey and always very curious. One hot
afternoon he heard, *Jingle-jingle. Jingle-jingle.* What could that

music be? George was curious about the melody he heard coming in through the window.

"That's an ice cream truck, George," said the man with the yellow hat. "You know summertime is here when you start hearing the music of the ice cream truck."

George loved trucks, and he loved ice cream. Ice cream would taste so good on a hot day like today! He would find this wonderful ice cream truck right away. He started to climb out of the window, but his friend stopped him. George had to finish his lunch first.

By the time George rushed out the door, the music was gone.

"Don't worry, George," the man said. "The ice cream truck

makes a trip around town each day, all summer long. We'll catch the ice cream truck tomorrow."

The next day it got hotter and hotter. George waited for the ice cream truck, but there was no sight or sound of it.

"Let's go to the pool, George," said the man with the yellow hat. George ran to get his towel. Splashing around in the pool would be a great way to beat the heat!

But the pool was closed for renovation.

"Look on the bright side, George. By autumn, we'll have a larger pool with three diving boards. Won't that be fun?" It did sound fun. But George needed to cool off now, not in the autumn!

So, George went back to waiting for the ice cream truck. He dreamed of vanilla, chocolate, and strawberry ice cream bars.

George thought he heard the music of the ice cream truck once . . .
but it was just a little boy's harmonica.

George and his neighbors decided to go to the park to run
through the sprinklers. But just as they arrived, the sprinklers
were turned off. It was a long walk back home.

Luckily for George, there was lemonade waiting for him on the porch. George took a drink and made a face. It was warm.

"Sorry, George," the man with the yellow hat said. "Our freezer has decided to stop working. All our ice cubes have melted." Now would be the perfect time to hear the sweet sound of the ice cream truck. Wait—was that it? Yes, there was the truck turning the corner now!

"Wave it down, George. I'll be right back with my wallet!" The man rushed back into the house. But the ice cream truck driver could not see the little monkey on the curb. The truck was not driving very quickly, but it was driving away!

George looked back at his house. He looked at the truck. Then
he had an idea. George climbed a tree and swung from branch to
branch until he swung right onto the roof of the truck. He rode the
truck into town. The truck stopped beside the town park. A window
on the side opened up, and a small child and her mother stopped to
buy ice cream.

George could not believe his eyes. The little girl had ordered
a frozen treat that looked exactly like a chocolate-covered banana!
George danced happily. He knew exactly what to order. The little
girl saw him and laughed.

So many people wanted ice cream that the driver ran out of change. He hurried over to the nearby bank to get more. Meanwhile, George noticed that the ice cream line was getting very long. Everyone looked hot. There was no shade to stand in. Maybe he could help.

George jumped down into the truck, where it was dark and cool. He grabbed as many ice cream bars, cones, and ice pops as he could. He handed them out to the waiting children, their parents . . . and even their pets! George worked so quickly, he didn't remember to collect money for the ice cream. No one seemed to mind—except the ice cream man!

"What have you done?" he cried when he returned. "Half my ice cream is gone!"

George was in trouble now. He climbed up a telephone pole. George was very glad to see his friend hurrying toward the park.

"Hold on a minute," said a voice below. "Look at how everyone is enjoying themselves! It's been the hottest summer in town history. An ice cream social is exactly what we need." It was the mayor, and she offered to pay for everyone's ice cream. "Thank you, George, for your great idea. I think the town should sponsor an ice cream party every summer!"

The ice cream truck driver was happy to keep serving ice cream. George and the man with the yellow hat helped.

The ice cream man saved one last treat for George—a chocolate-covered banana-cicle! It was the perfect treat for a curious monkey on a hot day!

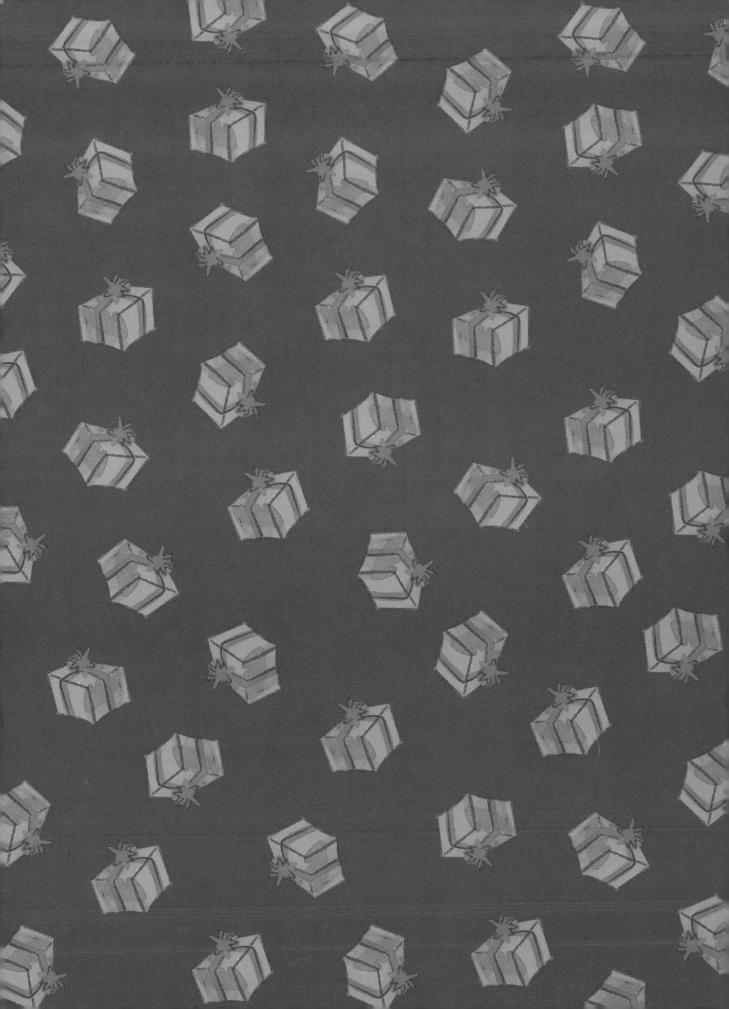

Curious George
and the Surprise Party

This is George. He was a good little monkey and always very curious.

One morning George and his friend made a long list of stores

to visit. They were throwing a party for their friend Charkie. The party

was going to be a surprise. George and the man went into town for supplies. They needed snacks, drinks, and decorations, too. Charkie was going to be so happy!

"Hello, Mrs. R.," the man said. George couldn't believe his eyes. It was their neighbor, Mrs. R., and Charkie was with her! "Hello, Charkie," the man said. "Isn't today your birthday? Happy birthday, Charkie."

George was nervous. He did not want to do anything to spoil Charkie's surprise.

"That was close, George," the man whispered. "I was scared I was

going to say something about the party and give away our surprise!"
George thought it was funny that he and the man had worried about
the same thing.

George and the man waved to all of their neighbors on the
walk. They saw the mail carrier, the police officer, and a bunch of
kids riding the school bus.

"It will be such a nice surprise for Charkie to find everyone at
our house tonight!" the man whispered again.

George and the man stopped at the fruit stand first. The stand had

lots of good things to eat: apples, cherries, cucumbers, and George's favorite—bananas. Mrs. R. and Charkie came too. Mrs. R. looped Charkie's leash over the fire hydrant while she did her shopping.

George knew Charkie loved oranges, so he decided to choose a few of those for the party. But, oh! When George picked up one orange,

the rest of the oranges tumbled after it! George was glad his favorite fruit was not a good shape for rolling. He helped put the oranges back as best he could and chose a bunch of bananas for his lunch.

The man was very busy saying hello to their friends from down the street. Mrs. R. was very busy choosing the shiniest apples. George was very busy examining the bananas. No one saw Charkie staring at the kitten. No one saw Charkie wriggle her leash loose from the hydrant. And no one, not even George, who was very good at noticing important things, saw Charkie dash off!

George, the man, and Mrs. R. walked to the post office to pick up some packages. The man had sent away for Charkie's birthday present. George knew it was a nice new collar. George thought Charkie would love the present Mrs. R. had sent away for—a whole box of sweet biscuit bones!

George thought he heard a *bark!* and a *meow!* outside the
post office. But he was thinking about how much Charkie would
like the bones and didn't wonder if the *bark!* could be Charkie's.

George, the man, and Mrs. R. went back to the fruit stand to meet up with Charkie. But when they arrived at Charkie's hydrant, George noticed something was wrong.

"Oh, no!" Mrs. R. said. "Charkie ran away!"

George felt awful. They could not have a party for Charkie if Charkie was missing. And what if they could not find her? Mrs. R. would be so sad. George would be sad too. George decided to look and look until he found Charkie.

He looked everywhere. Under the oranges at the fruit stand (they are Charkie's favorite). Behind the counter at the post office (maybe Charkie followed the scent of the biscuit bones there?). George could think of only one other thing Charkie liked better than oranges and biscuit bones. The park!

When George, the man, and Mrs. R. arrived at the park, they did not see Charkie. Had she burrowed in the sandbox? Was she hiding in the playhouse? Had she chased a squirrel up the tree? George looked and looked, but he couldn't find Charkie anywhere.

"Where could she be?" asked the man.

"What if we can't find her before nightfall?" asked Mrs. R. "I am so worried!"

But George thought he saw something. It looked like a little

bit of wagging tail poking out of the bushes.

"Charkie!" Mrs. R. said as George lifted a branch. And it

was her! Charkie was back, safe and sound.

"You did it, George," said the man. "You found Charkie and saved the day." George felt very happy.

That night, all their friends from the neighborhood came over to George's house. George and the man had set up everything for the party. When Charkie and Mrs. R. finally arrived, Charkie gave a big *yip!* of surprise.

"Happy birthday, Charkie!" they all sang. Mrs. R. smiled. The man scratched Charkie behind the ears. George gave Charkie a big monkey hug.

It was a perfect surprise party.

Curious George Learns to Count from 1 to 50

This is George. George was a good little monkey and always very curious. This morning George was curious about numbers. His friend, the man with the yellow hat, had been teaching him to count. Already George could count to five on one hand and ten on his two feet.

"Good job, George!" said his friend. "But you can count more than your fingers and toes. We're going into town today. I'll bet you can find lots of things to count along the way!"

The number 50 sounded like
a lot to George.

He was curious.
Could he find fifty
things to count?

First George counted his bed — **1**. Then he counted **2**
blankets. He tossed his pillows and counted **1, 2, 3**! He
counted **4** legs on his bed and **5** pull toys. What else could
George count?

Why, there were lots of things in the toy box!

There were **6** toy boats,

7 cars,

8 trucks,

9 stuffed animals,

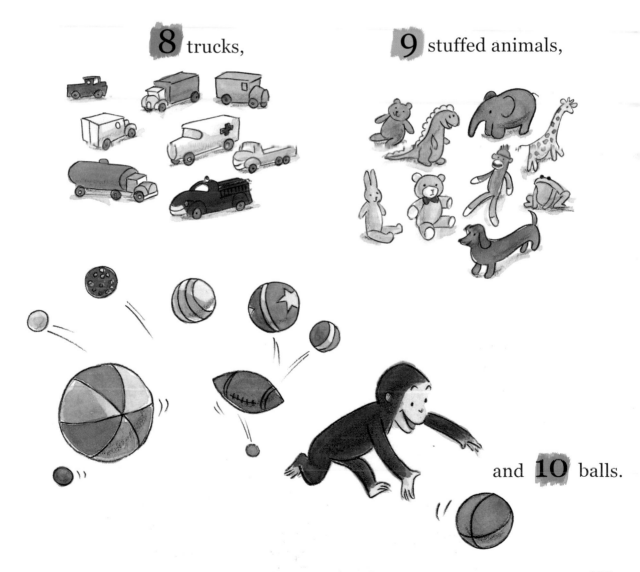

and **10** balls.

George followed one bouncing ball into his friend's room.
The man with the yellow hat was getting dressed. George wanted
to dress up, too!

He saw **11** hats to choose from,

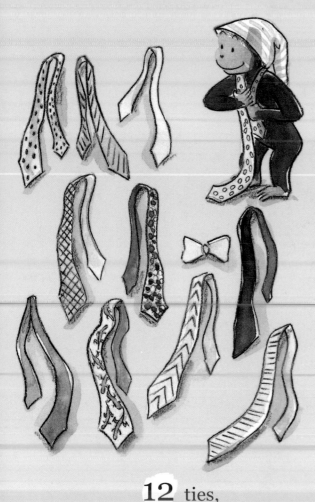
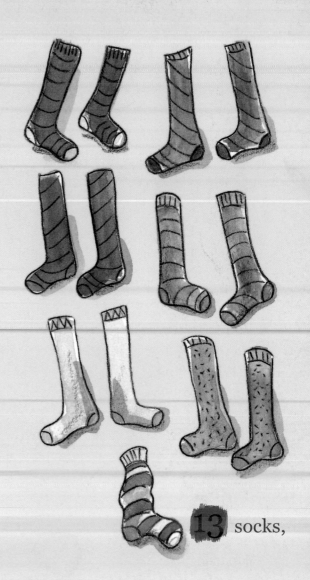

12 ties,   **13** socks,

and **14** shoes.

In the bathroom, George's friend had just finished brushing his teeth. "I'm going to make breakfast, George," he said. But George was still busy counting. He counted **15** blue tiles,

16 rubber ducks,

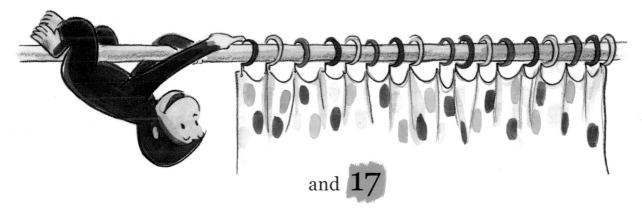

and **17**

shower rings.

It was fun to

count upside down!

Then George drew a surprise for his friend—

 **18** toothpaste pictures.

In the kitchen, George found more things to count.

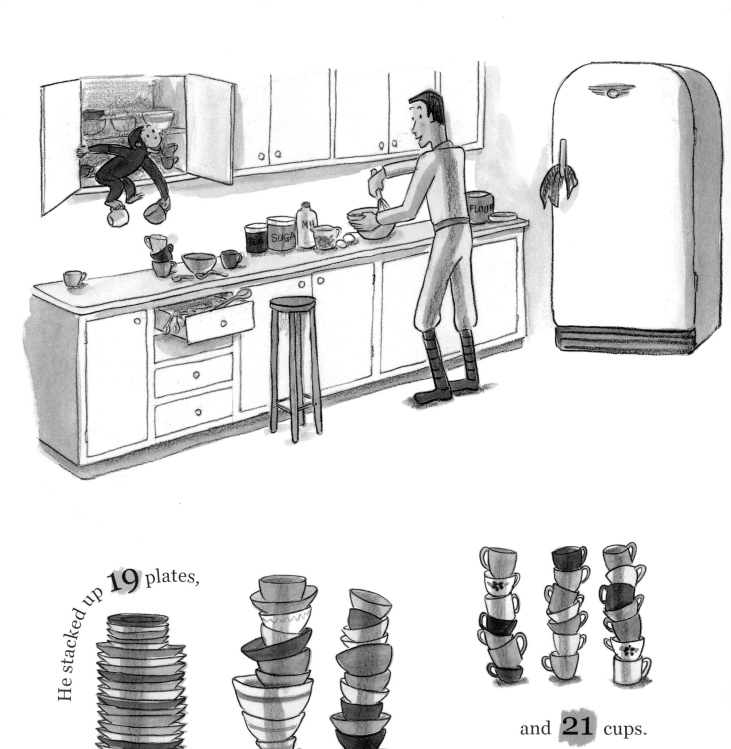

He stacked up **19** plates,

20 bowls,

and **21** cups.

He arranged **22** straws, **23** napkins,

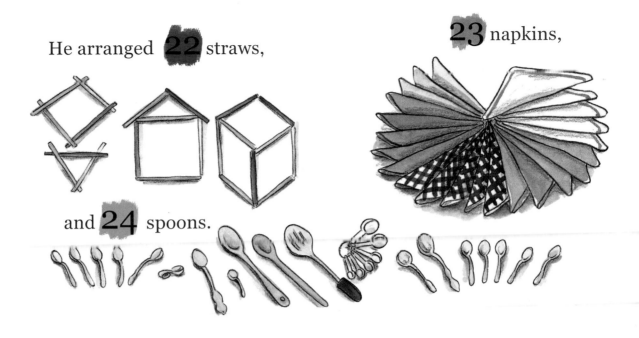

and **24** spoons.

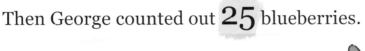

Then George counted out **25** blueberries.

"Don't forget to count our pancakes," the man said. George counted while his friend flipped— **26**!

When George was full and his plate was empty, he was ready to count outside.

In the backyard George counted **27** clouds floating by —

and **28** apples on a tree.

There was lots to do outside!

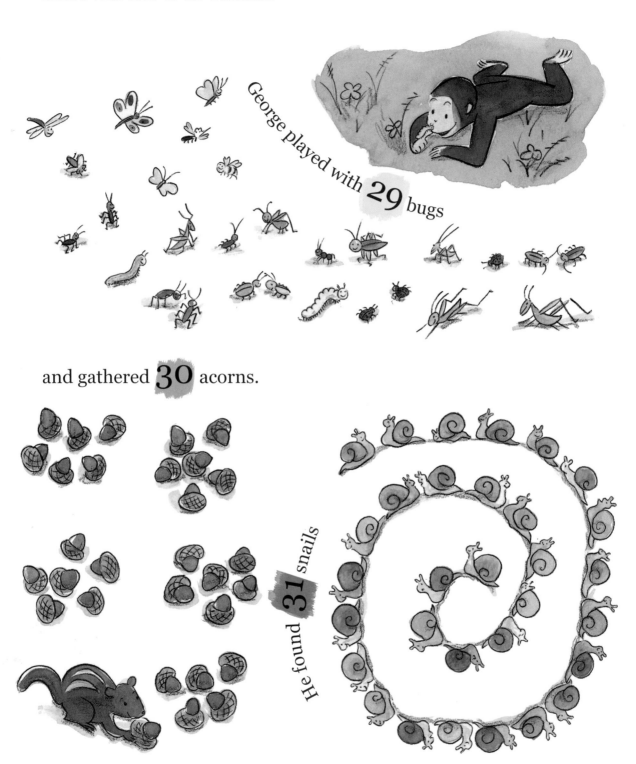

George played with **29** bugs

and gathered **30** acorns.

He found **31** snails

and arranged **32** sticks to create a design.

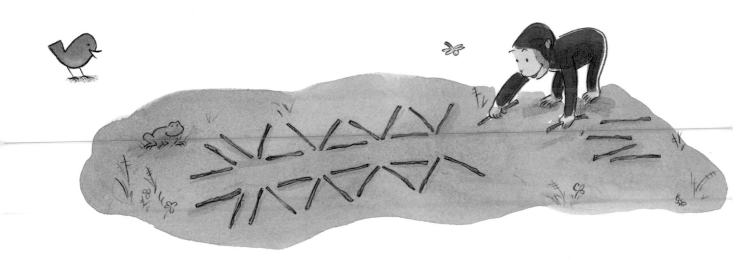

Then George smelled the daisies—and he picked **33**!

In his front yard George counted **34** noisy birds and **35** leaves blowing in the air. There was something else in the air—a gust of wind scattered **36** letters with colorful stamps! George counted as he helped pick them up.

"It's time to go into town, George," his friend said. "Do you remember how to walk there? You can lead the way."

George, curious as ever, took the long way from his house to town! As he walked, he counted **37** houses, **38** chimneys, and **39** trees. Can you follow George's path through his neighborhood?

In town, George and his friend saw workers fixing up a building.

There was a very tall ladder—and George could not resist!

He scampered up **40** rungs past **41** windows.

What a view! From up on top of the ladder, George counted

42 people. One of them was his friend Betsy!

"Hi, George," Betsy said when he climbed down to see her.

"Your friend told me you are learning to count."

Then George walked Betsy to her school.

"Why don't you come inside?" she asked him. "There are

lots of things to count in here!"

Betsy was right. There were plenty of things to count in her class-

room!

While George's friend talked to the teacher . . .

George counted **43** sparkly beads,

44 jars of paste,

and **45** crayons.

On the table **46** colorful feathers were laid out. George

was curious—what were they for?

Betsy's classmates were making hats and decorations for a special celebration. George wanted to make decorations, too.

In fact, he turned himself into a decoration!

Then George's new friends cleaned off **47** colored strips of paper—and a lot of glue!

"George is counting all the way to fifty," Betsy said.

Susan said, "We can help! How about counting paperclips?"

She and her sister Sarah helped George find 48.

A moment later the bell rang and everyone was on the move. George counted **49** wheels. Then it was time for him to go home, too . . .

George ran and ran. He ran **50** steps—all the way back to the man with the yellow hat!

His friend was so happy to see him. "You did it, George!" his friend said proudly. "You used your own two feet to count all the way up to fifty!"

About the Creators

Hans Augusto Rey (1898–1977) met his wife-to-be, Margret (1906–1996), at a party in her father's home in Germany; when he first caught a glimpse of her, she was sliding down the banister. In their twenties and thirties they lived in Paris and Rio de Janeiro, Brazil, where Hans sold bathtubs up and down the Amazon River. The Reys eventually settled in Cambridge, Massachusetts, and Waterville Valley, New Hampshire.

Throughout their lives the Reys created many lively picture books together, including *Spotty, Cecily G. and the Nine Monkeys,* and *Pretzel,* and lift-the-flap books such as *How Do You Get There?* But it is their incorrigible little monkey, Curious George, who has become an American icon and captured the hearts of readers everywhere.

Original Curious George Stories by Margret and H. A. Rey:

Curious George

Curious George Takes a Job

Curious George Rides a Bike

Curious George Gets a Medal

Curious George Flies a Kite

Curious George Learns the Alphabet

Curious George Goes to the Hospital